Usborne

100 Birds to Fold & Fly

Illustrated by Kat Leuzinger

Designed by Hannah Ahmed
and Brian Voakes

Turn over for tips on folding,
flying and looking after
your paper birds.

Useful tips

Here are some helpful tips that will make your birds fly more effectively and keep them in good condition.

How to launch your paper bird

Follow these steps for a perfect take-off and landing:

- Stand facing forward.

- Hold each bird just in front of the middle of its body.

- Pull back and then throw forward in a long, smooth movement to release your bird.

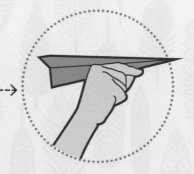

Folding

- Place a ruler along the folds and press down to keep them sharp.

- If you want to keep your bird for another day, store it flat inside a book.

- If your bird gets wet, or won't fly... fold a new one!

Flying

- Try changing the angle of your bird's wings to alter its flight.

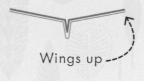

Wings up

Wings down

Add a wing tip fold

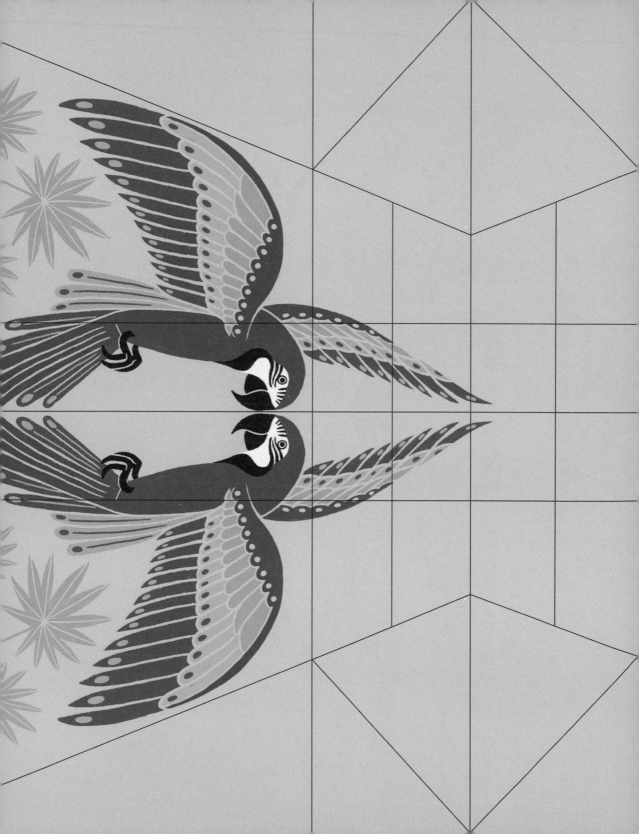

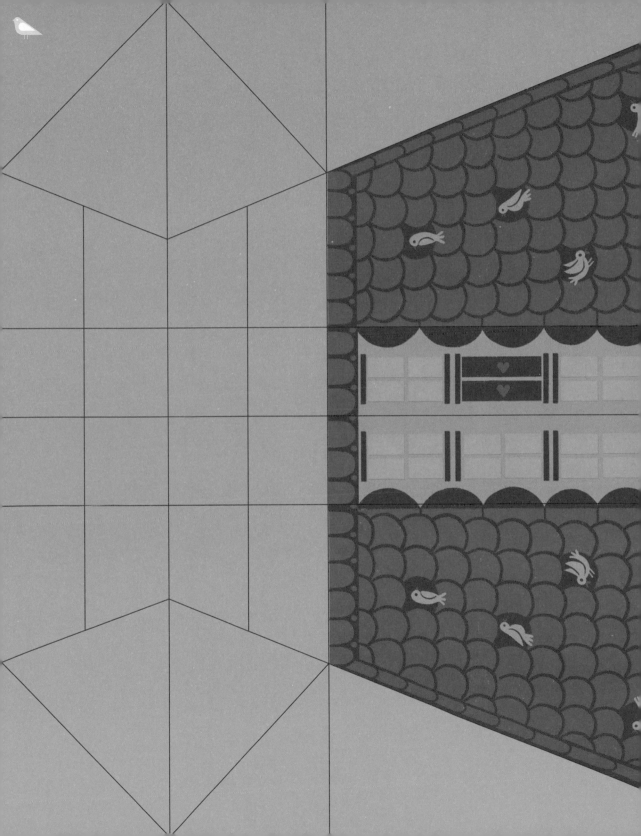

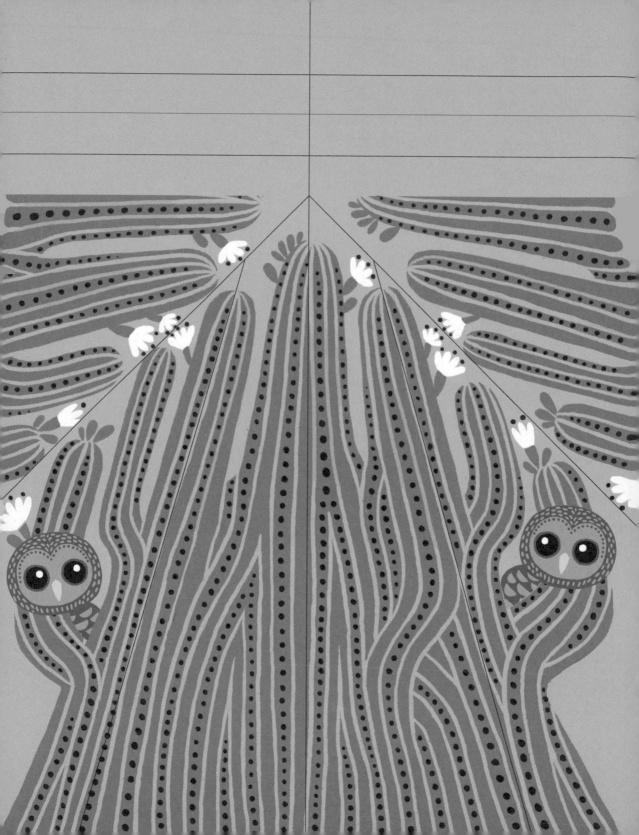

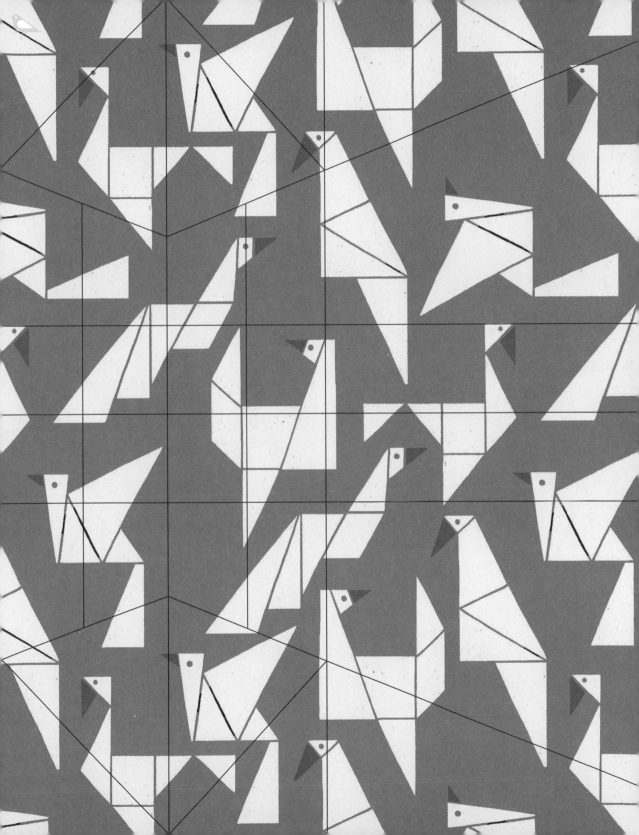

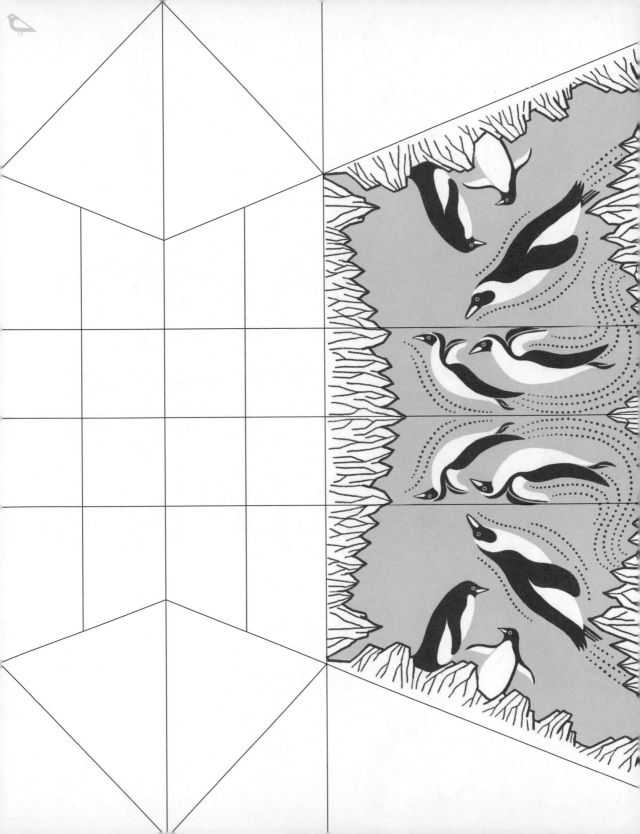

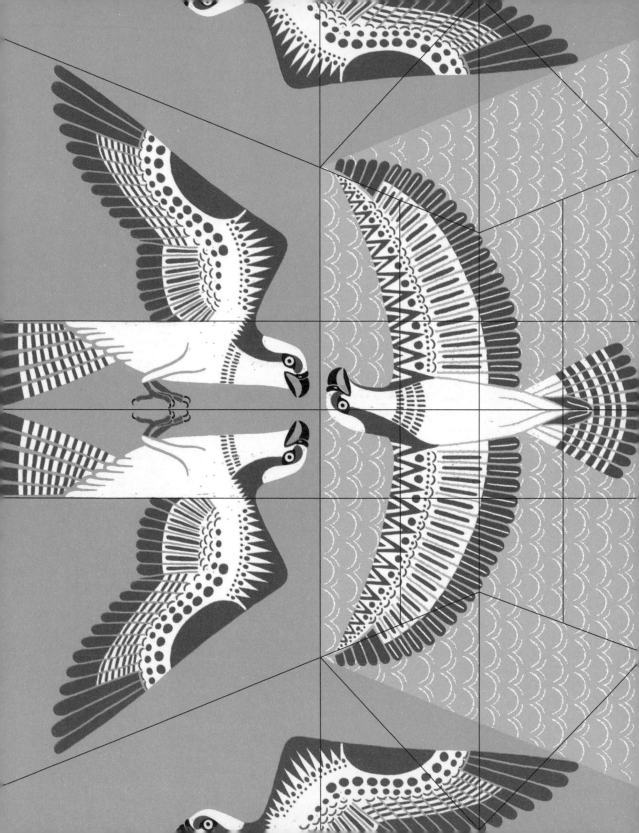

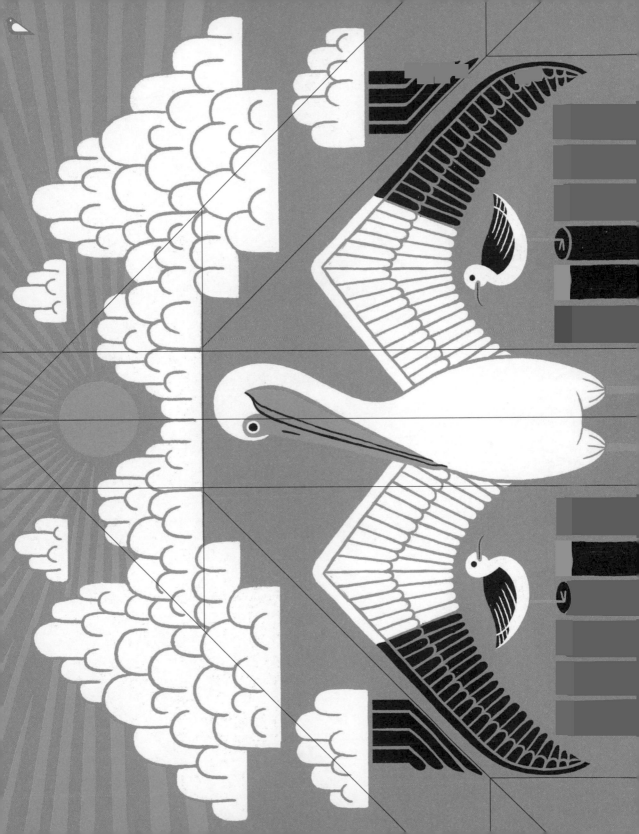

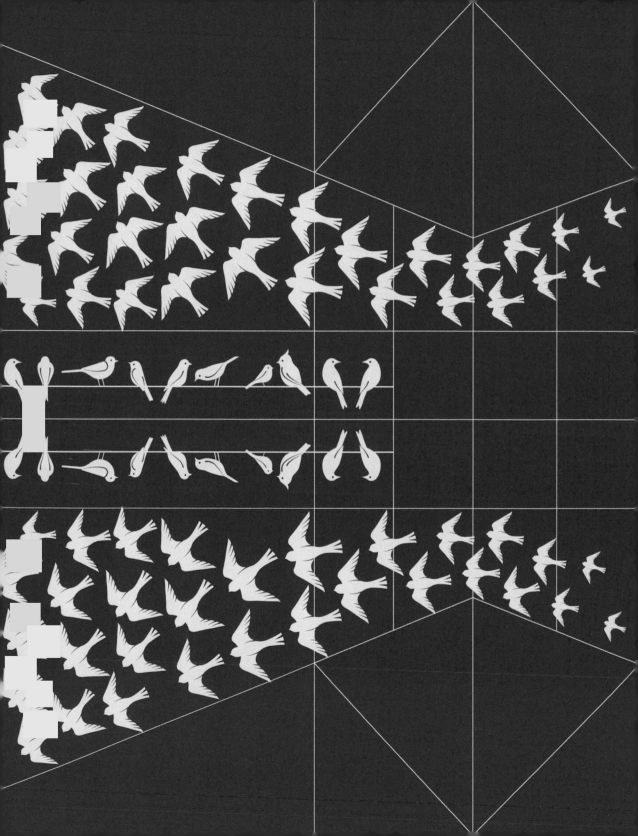

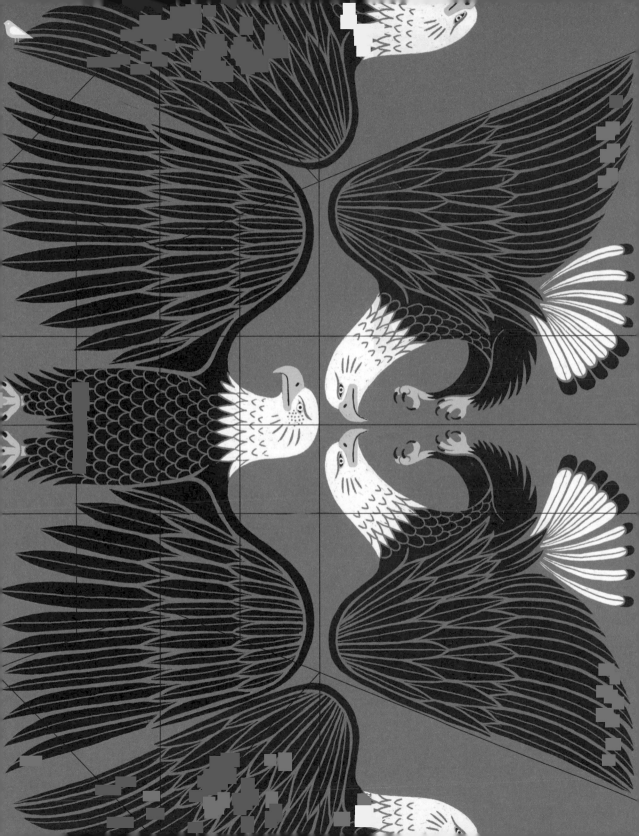

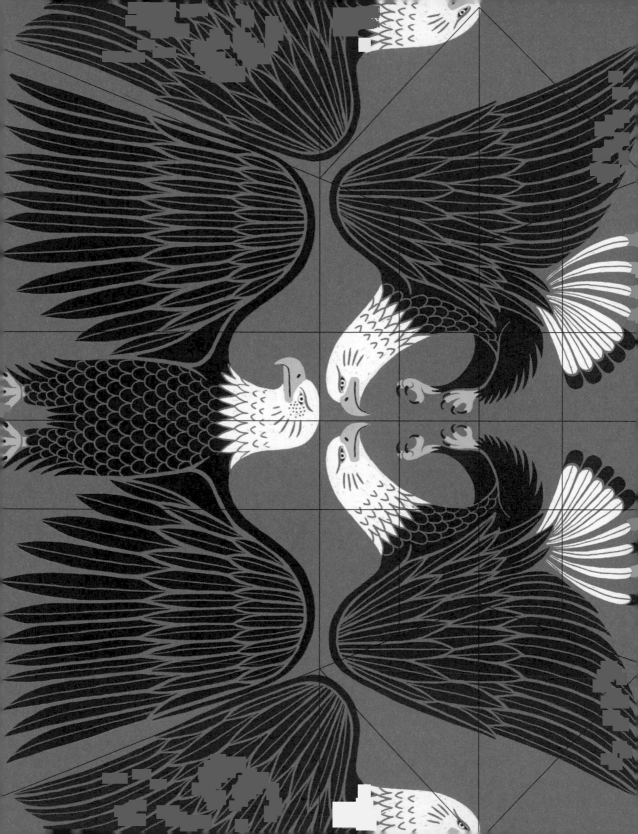

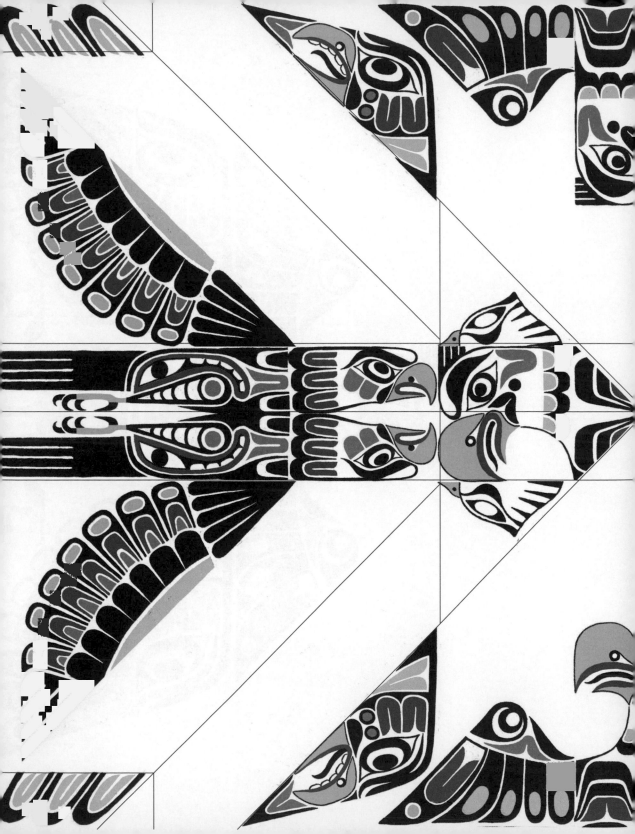

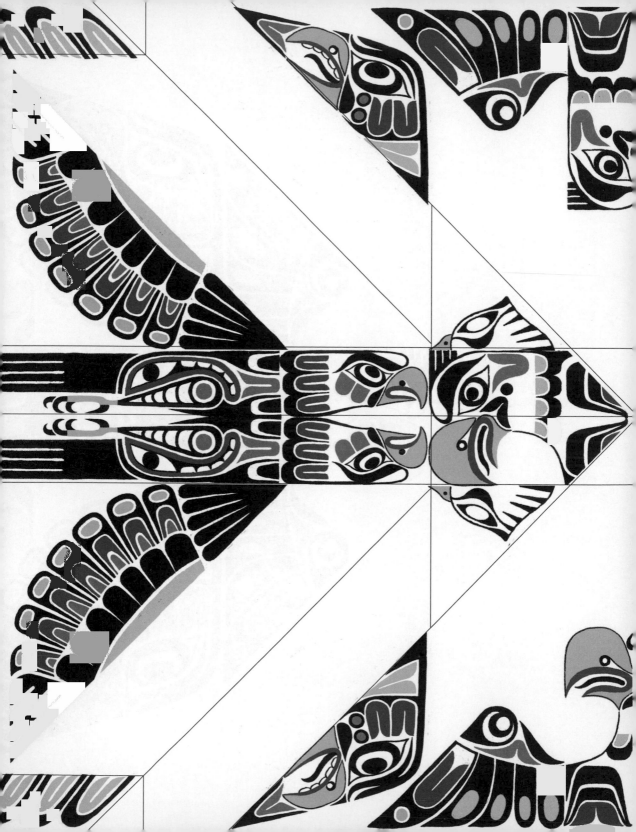

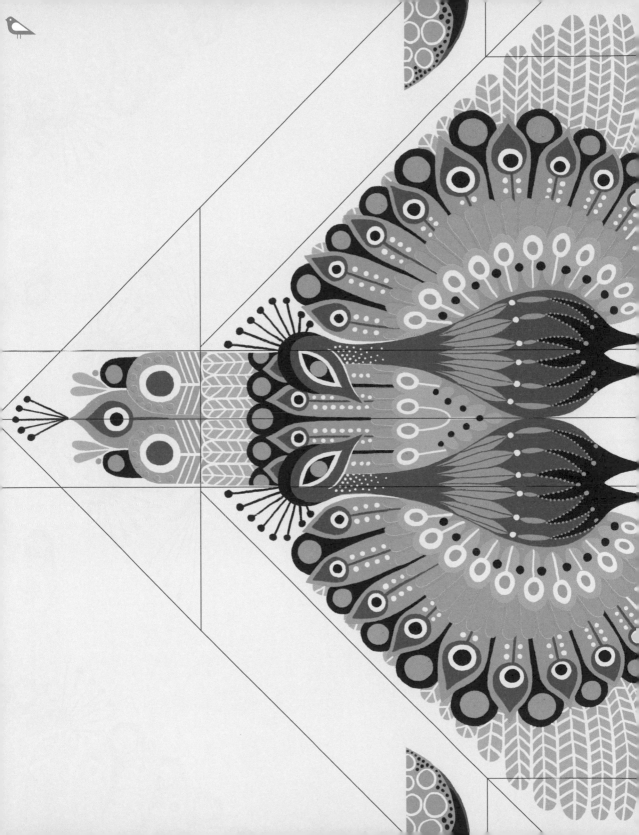

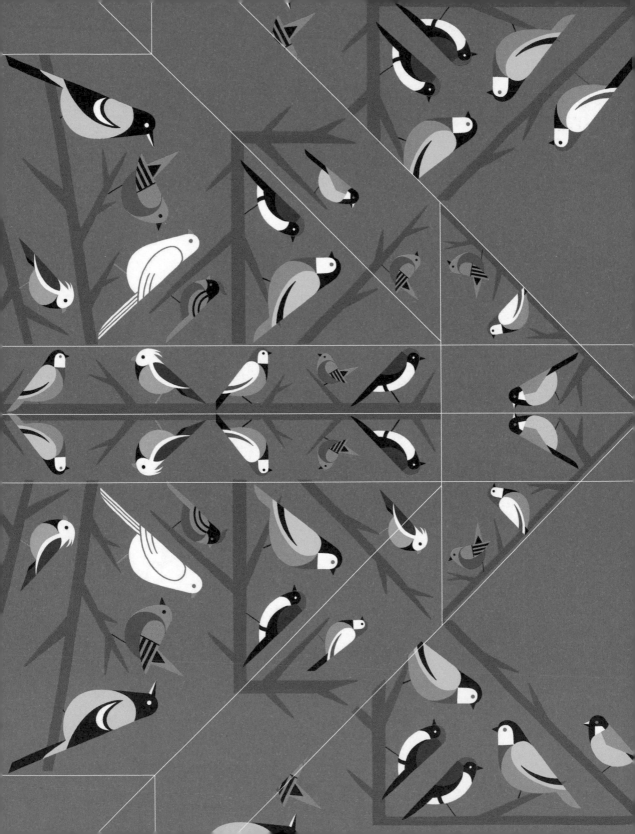

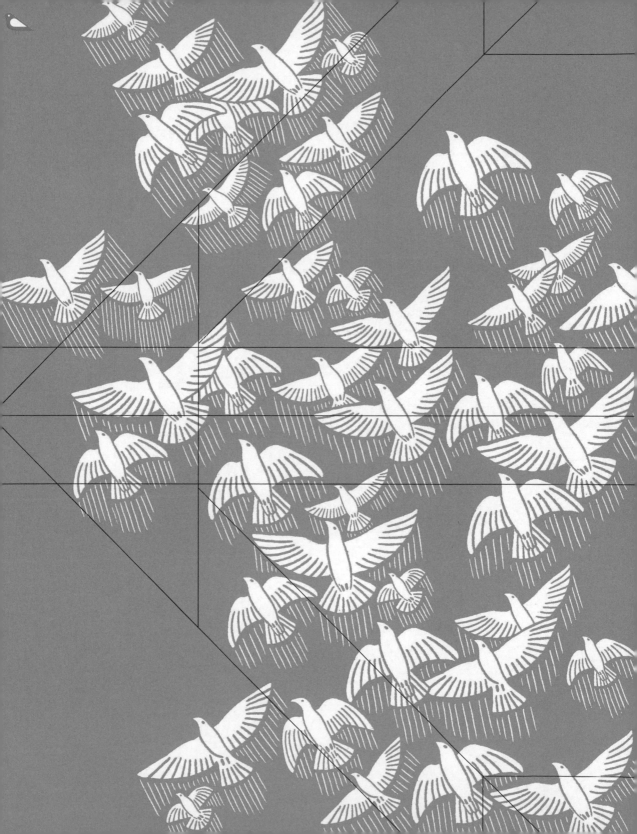

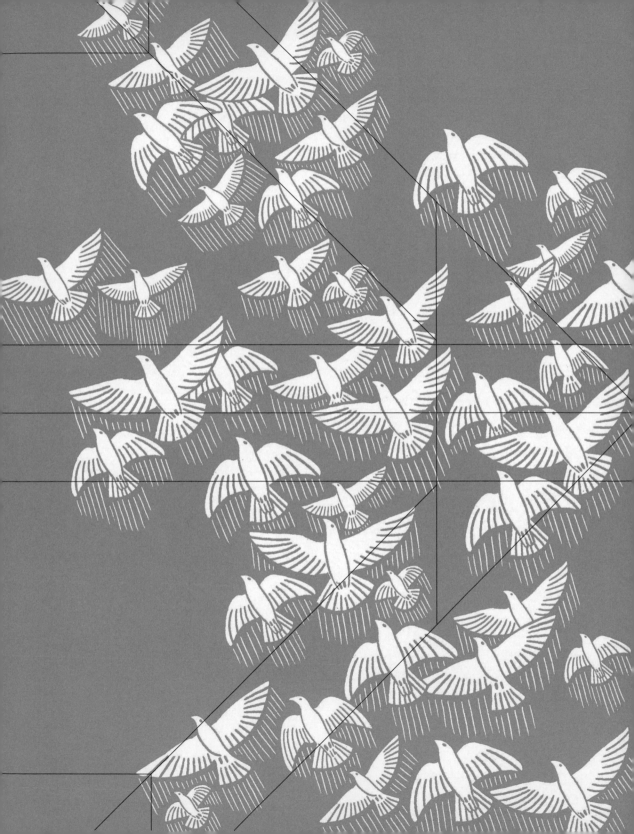

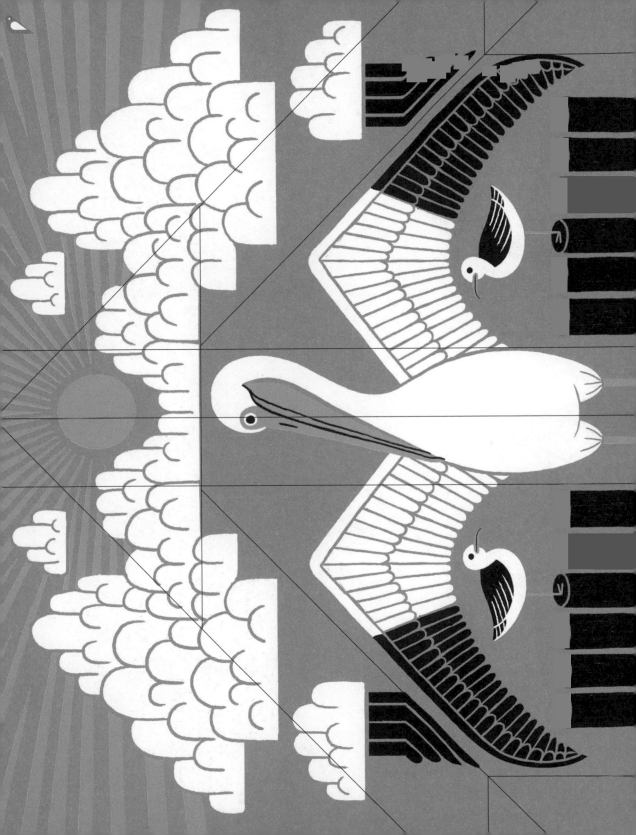

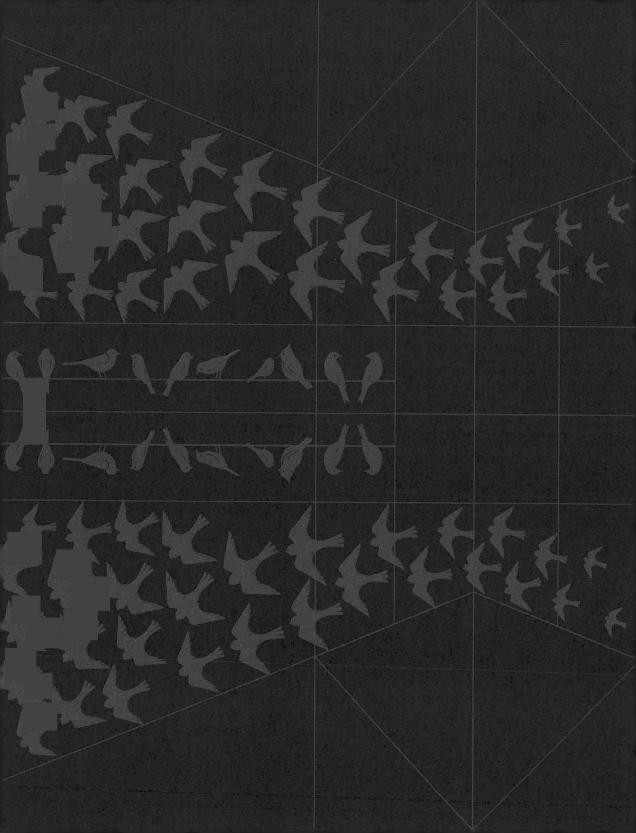

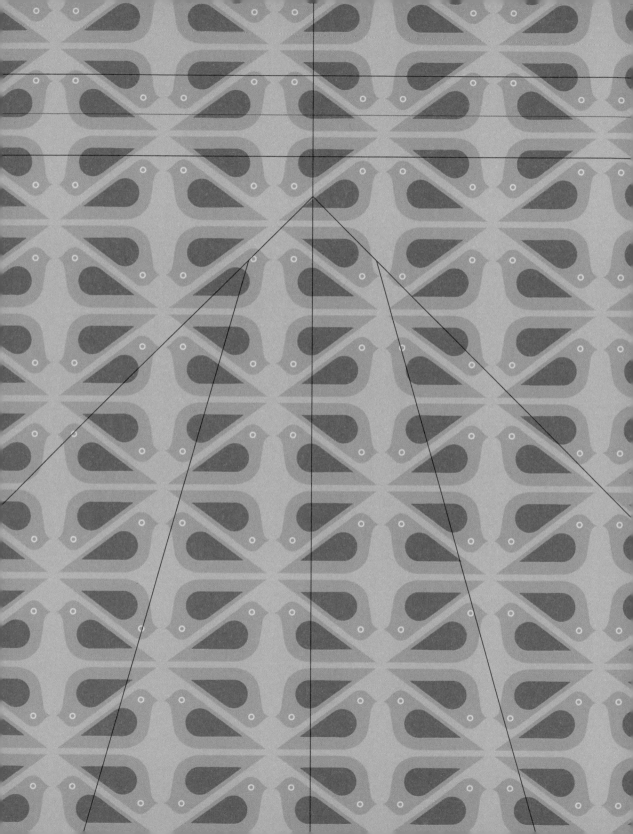

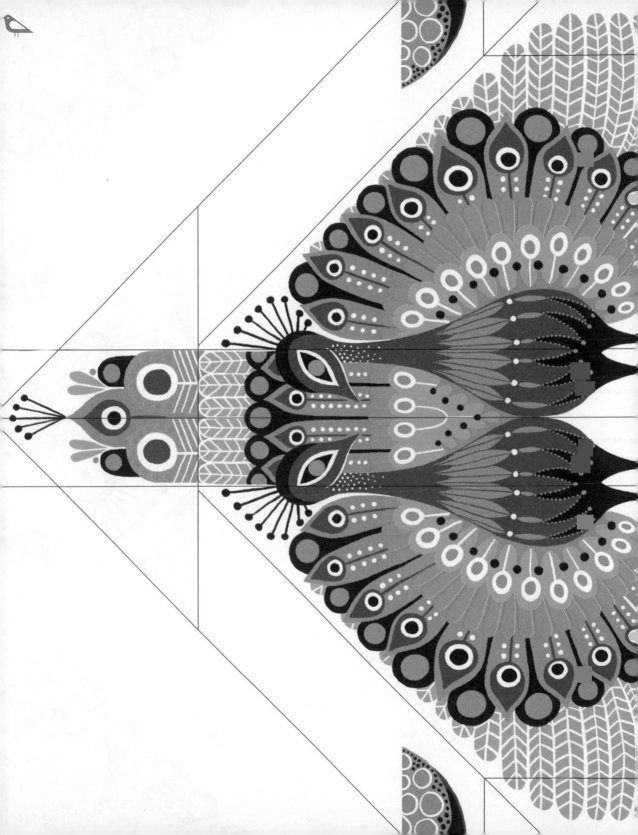

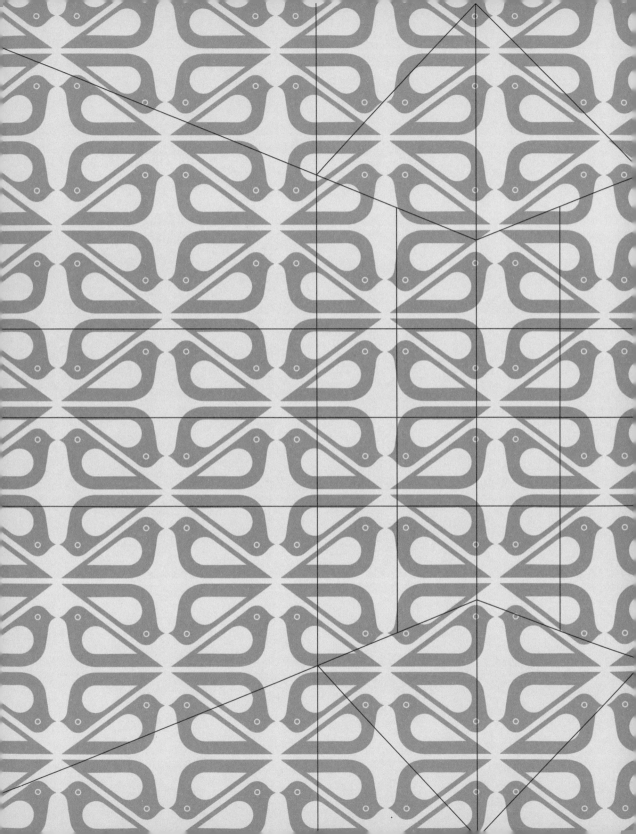

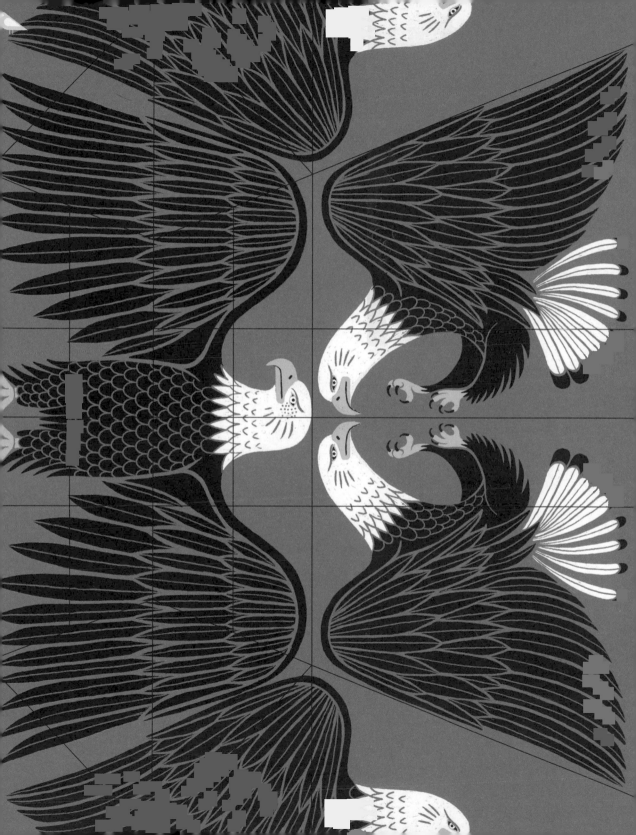

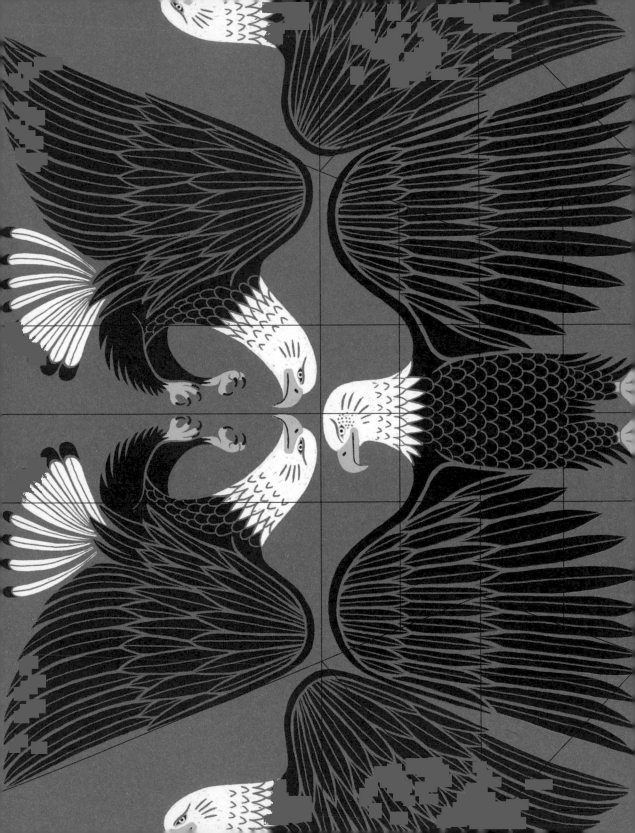

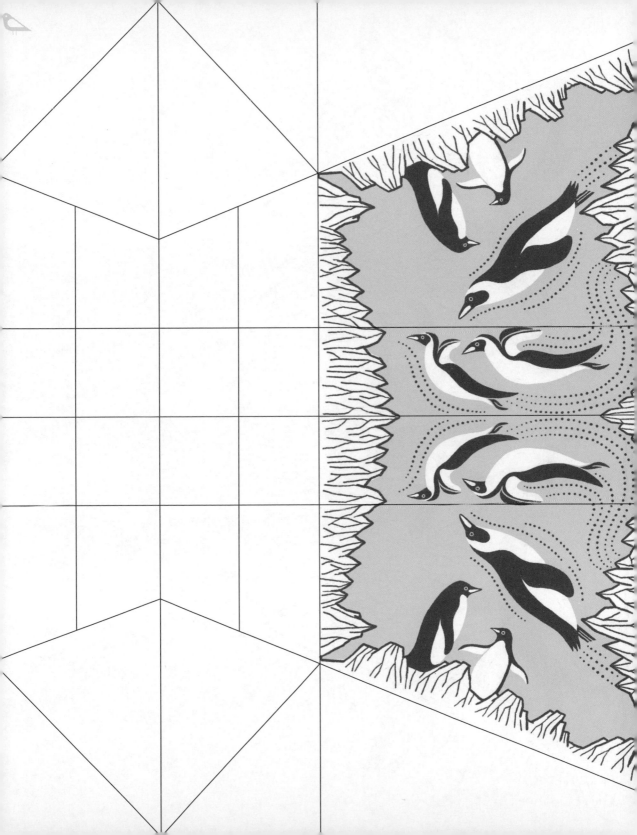

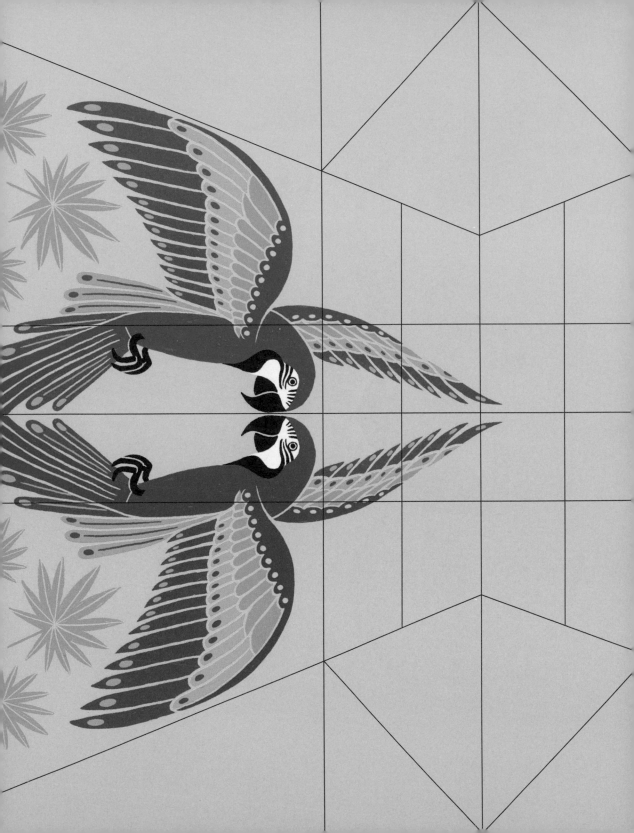

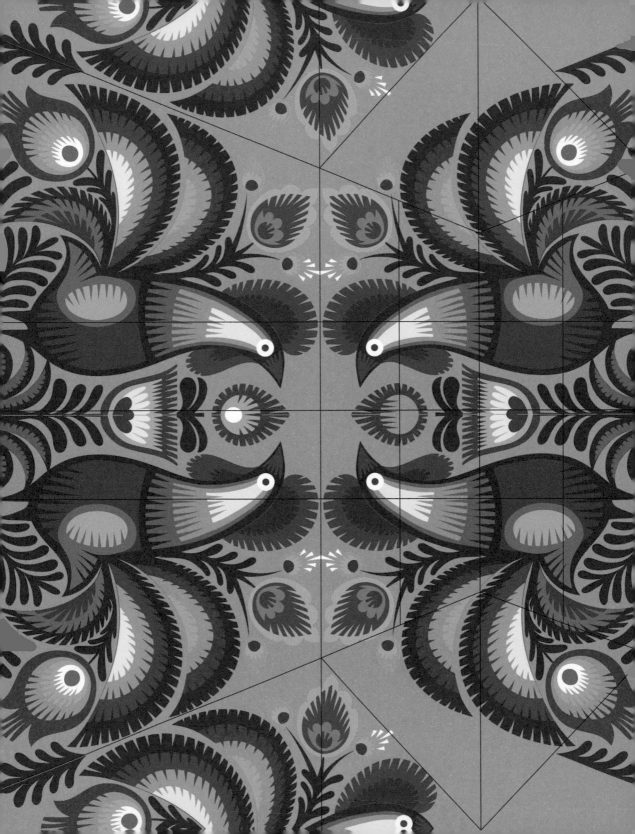

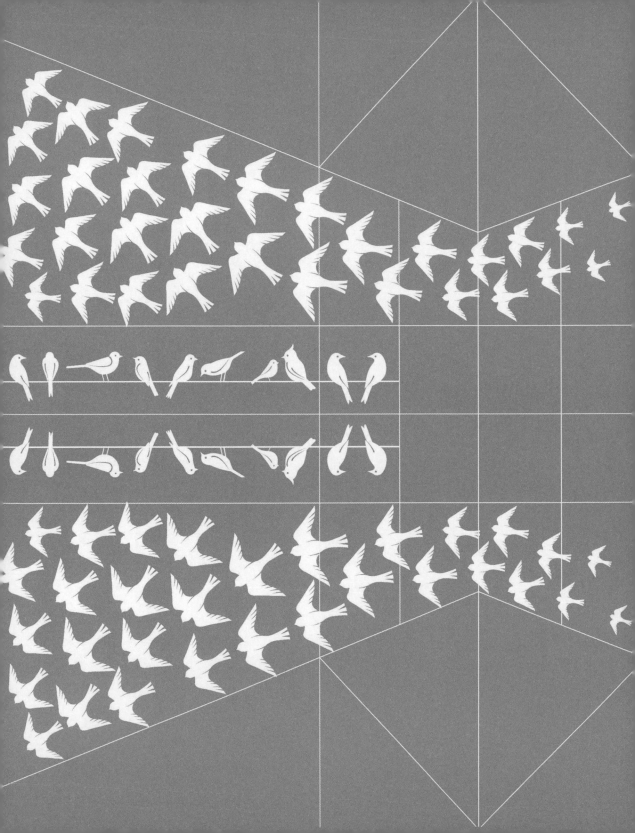

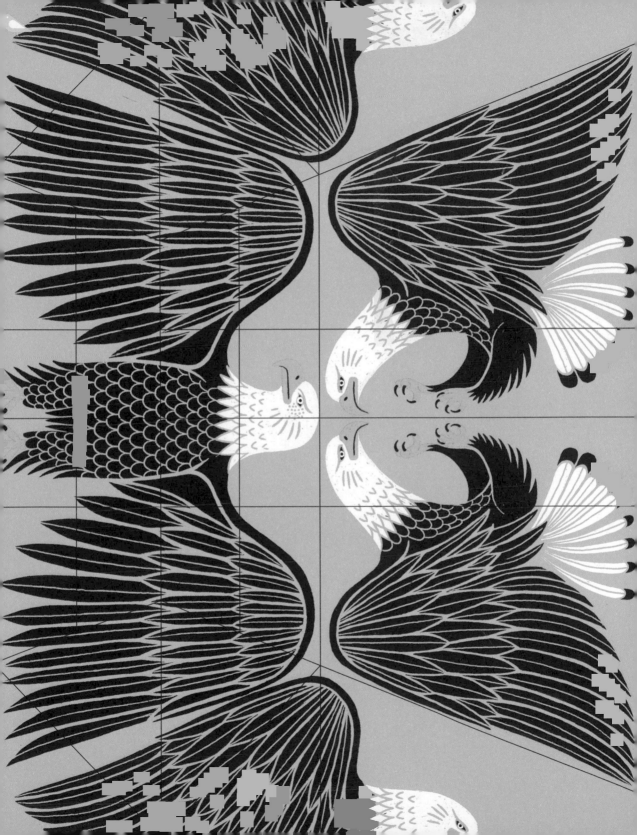

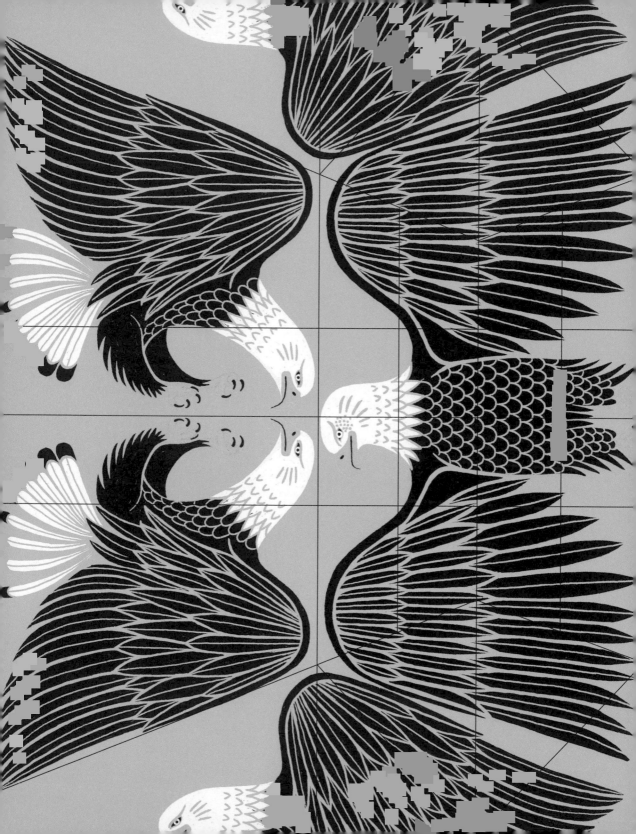

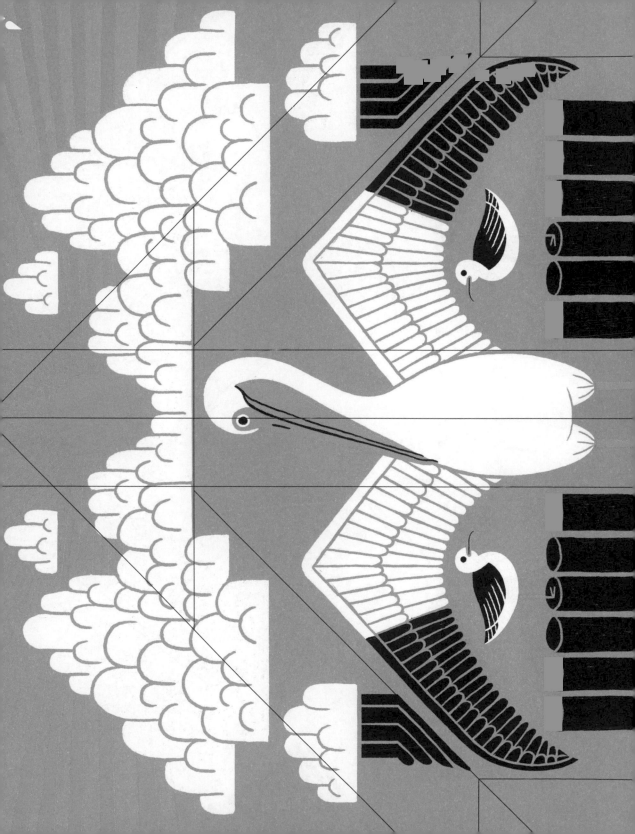

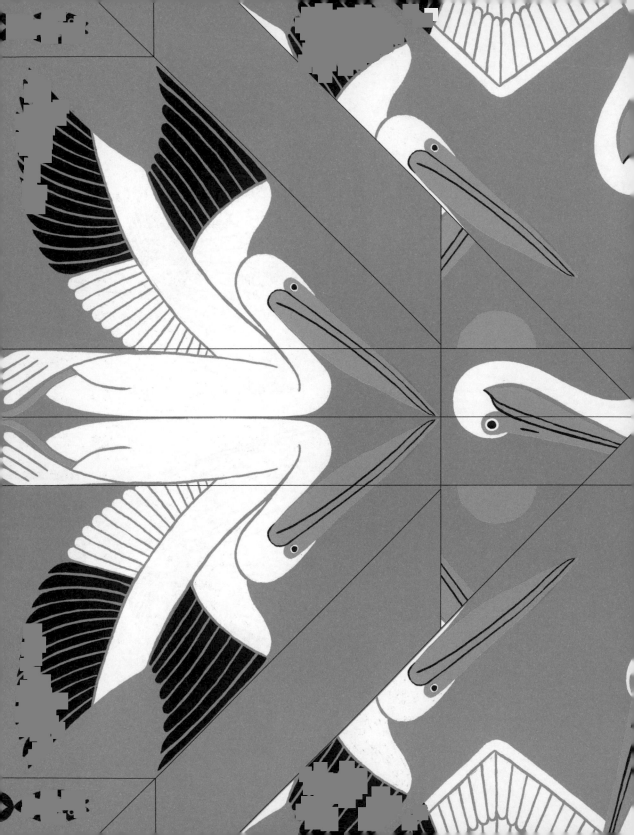

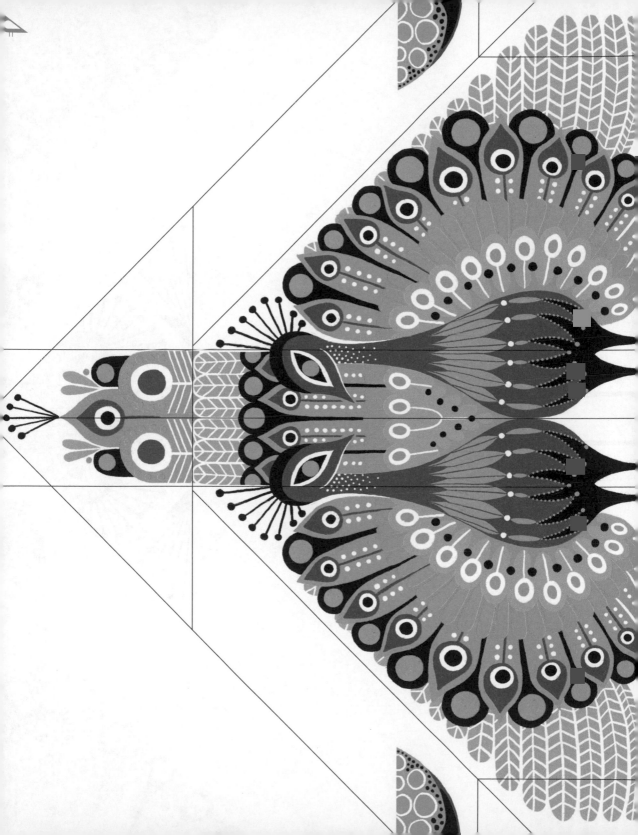

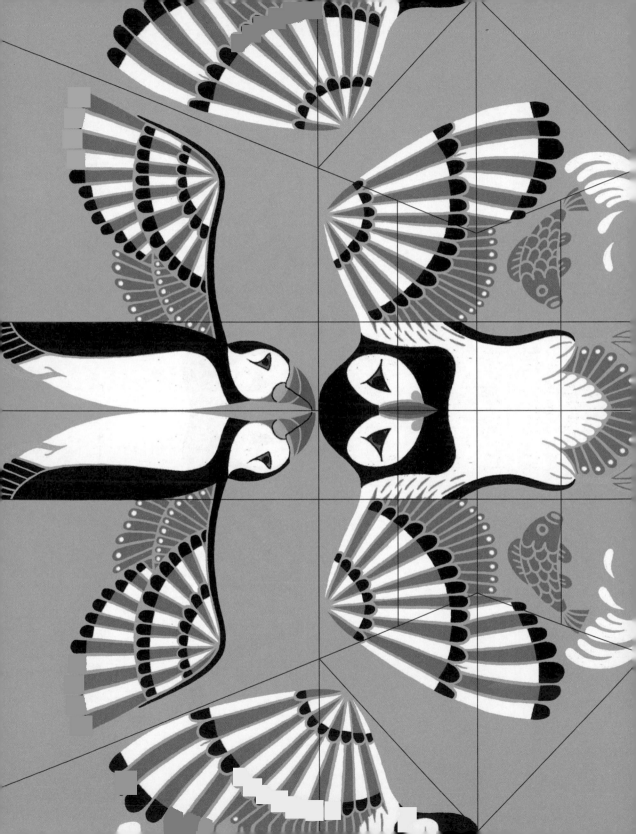